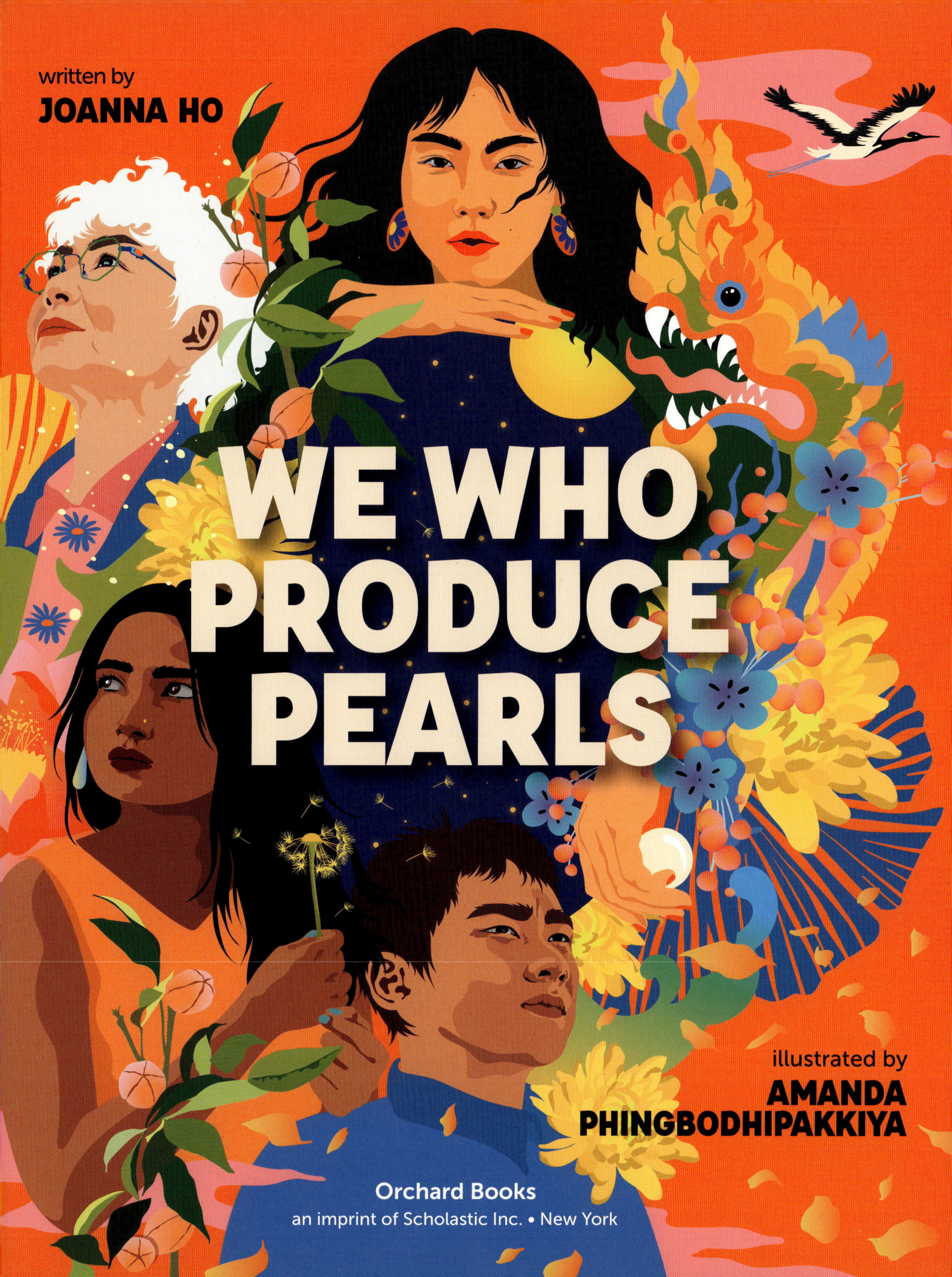

We who cultivate
      come from homes and histories
      diverse as the gardens of
        orchids and hibiscus,
          marigolds and plumeria,
           peonies and plum blossoms
blanketing our lands in rich tapestries of color.

When they came for that which was not theirs,
      sowing toxic flowers that bloomed in midair,
we held their injustice in our mouths.

We came in shackles on ships.
We came swindled into servitude.
We came clutching ideas and aspirations.

We who persist
 are the wealth
  and riches of the world.
We hold empires upon our backs
 and wear crowns
  covered in jewels.

We are the water that coaxed spring
 shoots from the soil.
We are the tracks that connected sea
 to shining sea.
We are the gold that fed the dreams
 of a generation.

Our battered bodies become battle cries for justice.
We shout no-no at the system
　　that paints freely with our blood
　　　　but shuts its eyes to our rights.
We hold injustice in our mouths,
　　encircle it with tenacity and audacity,
　　and roll it around on our tongues.

We who stand in solidarity
   understand the vines of freedom
      must climb arbors of cooperation
     to bear fruits of liberation.

We work together on the line
   shielding each other with our fists and our fury,
    claiming space
      for our stories
        and dreams.

We who shine
 have the power to define
 the legacies we leave.
The truths we speak today
 pin themselves to the heavens
 in constellations
 that will guide the seekers
 of tomorrow.

. . . and spit it out.

We are children of the celestial.
We catch the light
and lead with brilliance so bright
we rechart the course
of the world.

An Invitation to Dig Deeper and Continue Learning

Each stanza in this book speaks to the shared histories of Asians in America. Each verse is inspired by specific figures, events, and movements in Asia and across the Asian diaspora. We represent a diversity of nationalities, languages, and cultures, yet we have more in common than we are often taught to see.

The decision to focus only on Asian Americans instead of also attempting to include rich Native Hawaiian and Pacific Islander stories came after listening to their communities. While we are often grouped together and our histories intertwined, we did not desire to replicate dynamics of oppression and erasure too often present in our intercommunity coalitions. It is important that Native Hawaiians and Pacific Islanders tell their own stories.

This is a resource to help you step beyond these pages to draw lines between the past, present, and future. Remember, it barely scratches the surface of all there is to learn. Don't stop here!

We who dream
Guiding Questions
- What is the significance of the moon in many Asian cultures?
- What is the symbolism of the sun across many Asian cultures?

Starting Points
- Chuseok, Hmong New Year, Lunar New Year, Tết, Losar
- Diwali
- Eid
- Loi Krathong
- Mid-Autumn Festival, Tsukimi
- Ramadan
- Nyepi
- Vaisakhi, Songkran, Puthandu
- National flags
- Feng Shui

We who seek
Guiding Question
- What circumstances caused people across Asia to migrate abroad?

Starting Points
- Aboriginal Taiwanese voyagers of 5000–1500 BC
- Explorer Ma He (馬和), also known as Zheng He (鄭和) in the early 1400s
- Filipino and Chinese sailors manning the Spanish galleons in the 1500s
- Legendary female pirate, Shi Yang (石陽), also known as Zheng Yi Sao (鄭一嫂) in the early 1800s

We who cultivate
Guiding Questions
- What are some of the similarities and differences in meaning of these flowers across Asian cultures: chrysanthemum, lotus, hibiscus, marigold, orchid, peony, plum blossom, plumeria?
- Where can you find them throughout this book? What is their significance?

When they came for that which was not theirs

Guiding Questions
- Why did imperialist and colonialist countries have interest in Asia?
- How were the overt and covert actions of Western imperialist and colonialist countries connected across Asia? What were the immediate impacts? What have been the lasting impacts in Asia? How do we continue to feel the impact in the United States today?
- How have imperialism and colonization created mass migration to the Americas?

Starting Points
- The Trans-Pacific slave trade of the 1500s
- "The other Middle Passage" of the 1800s and early 1900s
- Find the connections between:
  – The atomic bombs dropped in Japan
  – Napalm and Agent Orange used in Vietnam
  – The CIA, the Hmong, and the Secret War
  – The Plain of Jars in Laos
  – The killing fields of Cambodia
- Japanese colonization of Korea and China
- Escaping the impacts of imperialism and colonization:
  – Chinese people came during the Gold Rush to escape ravages of British-induced opium and Western trade forced upon the country after the Opium Wars in the mid-1800s.
  – Japanese people came during the Meiji Restoration, which began as a protective measure against the United States and European nations forcing Japan to trade with threat of war in late 1800s to early 1900s.
  – Koreans came to escape Japanese colonization and the plague in the early 1900s.
  – Indians came to escape the dislocation and high taxes caused by British colonization in the 1800s to early 1900s.
  – Vietnamese, Cambodian, Hmong, and Laotians came to escape the destruction and danger caused by United States–backed wars in their homelands.
- Our bodies are not our own: The history and stories of Asian women

We are the history of this land

Guiding Questions
- Why is it important to understand Asian American history as an essential part of the history of the United States?
- Why is Asian history inseparable from US history?

Starting Points
- Waves of Asian immigrants laid the foundation of irrigation projects and the agricultural revolution in the Central Valley, California.
- Ah Bing: Cultivator of the Bing cherry
- Lue Gim Gong: "The Citrus Wizard" and creator of today's Valencia orange
- George Shima: "The Potato King" who at one point produced 85% of California's potato crop

We who survive

Guiding Questions
- In what ways have the narratives about Asians shifted over time?
- Why have narratives about Asians changed?
- How have these shifting narratives impacted inter-Asian relations? Interracial relations?
- Who does this serve?
- Why is it important for Asians and Asian Americans to write our own narratives?

Starting Points
- The labels they give us: "yellow peril," "coolies," "little brown brothers," "dirty Japs," "gooks," "model minorities," "perpetual foreigners," "gang members," "unassimilable refugees," "terrorists," "dragon ladies," "tiger moms," "kung flu"
- Waves of Asian laborers brought in to expand sugar plantations in Hawaii were then used by white colonizers to foment anti-Asian sentiment and the illegal overthrow of Hawaii's constitutional government.
- 700 Filipino workers walked out of their agricultural jobs in 1933 and growers brought in other Asian immigrants and Mexicans as strikebreakers.
- "Chinese friends" vs. "Enemy Japs" during WWII turned quickly into support for Japan and anti-China rhetoric for economic benefit after the war.
- The deployment of the model minority myth during the civil rights movement
- The modern legal history of Asian immigration and exclusion:
  - Chinese Exclusion Act of 1882
  - Treaty of Paris of 1898
  - Gentlemen's Agreement of 1907
  - Continuous Journey Regulation of 1908
  - Immigration Act of 1917
  - Asian Exclusion Act of 1924
  - Tydings-McDuffie Act of 1934
  - Luce-Celler Act of 1946
  - McCarran-Walter Act of 1952
  - Immigration and Nationality Act of 1965
  - American Homecoming Act of 1989
  - Antiterrorism and Effective Death Penalty Act of 1996
  - Executive Order 13769 or the "Muslim Ban" of 2017

We who withstand

Guiding Question
- How did Asian immigrants build community despite hostile conditions in the United States?

Starting Points
- Manilamen of Saint Malo, Louisiana, in the late 1700s
- Chinatowns, "Nihonmachi" cooperatives, Korean churches
- Interracial communities:
  - Bengali Harlem
  - Punjabi-Mexican community of Imperial Valley, California
- Chinese Cuban communities in New York City
- Moksad Ali and Ella Blackman of New Orleans

We who persist

Guiding Questions
- How have colonizers built empires on the backs of Asian resources and labor?
- How were/are native communities impacted by colonial empire building?
- Colonizers have a pattern of coveting Asian culture and goods, while dehumanizing Asian people. Why do you think this is?
- What wealth and riches did Asians create and/or possess that brought foreign powers to our shores? What wealth and riches do we create and/or possess today?

Starting Points
- "Chinamania" of the 1800s
- A brief history of tea: China, Opium War, England, Boston Tea Party, Revolutionary War, ships sail for China from the United States the same day another ship sails to London to deliver the articles of peace at the end of the Revolutionary War
- India was referred to as the "bread basket" and "jewel in the crown" of the British colonies.
- Asian labor played a key role in:
   – The Transcontinental Railroad
   – Sugar plantations on the Hawaiian and Caribbean islands
   – Logging industries in the Pacific Northwest
   – Mines during the Gold Rush
   – Fishing ships and canneries along the Pacific coast and in Alaska
   – Laundromats and restaurants (work white workers refused)
- Tie Sing: a cook who worked for the United States Geological Survey on backcountry expeditions vital to the establishment of the National Park System

We who sacrifice

Guiding Questions
- How have Asians laid down our lives for justice?
- How has violence against Asians galvanized social movements?

Starting Points
- Some examples of anti-Asian lynching and mob violence:
   – October 1871: Los Angeles, CA, the largest mass lynching in US history
   – February 1885: Eureka, CA
   – November 1885: Tacoma, WA
   – September 1907: Bellingham, WA
- 442nd Regimental Combat Team also known as the Purple Heart Battalion during World War II
- No-No Boys
- Vincent Chin
- "America's most lethal weapon": Hmong soldiers in the Secret War
- Balbir Singh Sodhi
- Filipinx frontline healthcare workers during COVID
- Atlanta Spa Shooting victims: Delaina Ashley Yaun, Xiaojie Tan, Daoyou Feng, Paul Andre Michels, Hyun Jung Grant, Suncha Kim, Soon Chung Park, Yong Ae Yue
- Vicha Ratanapakdee

We who resist

Guiding Question
- How have Asians challenged prevailing systems to fight for justice and equality?

Starting Points
- Yick Wo: Won a case before the Supreme Court which ruled that prejudicial administration of a race-neutral law is an infringement of the Equal Protection Clause of the Fourteenth Amendment
- Mary and Joseph Tape: Sued the San Francisco school board for their daughter's right to public education
- Wong Kim Ark: Prevailed at the Supreme Court for birthright citizenship
- Sieh King-King: Spoke against the slave girl system and introduced feminist ideas to Chinatown
- Paper Sons: The first to be barred, Asians were also the first to devise their own systems of entering the United States
- Tarak Nath Das: Organized for Indian independence from the British
- The poetry of Angel Island Immigration Station
- Bhagat Singh Thind: Fought for Indian rights to US citizenship at the Supreme Court
- Fred Oyama: Struck down laws that prohibited Japanese people from owning land
- Viet Thanh Nguyen: Teaches literature and shares stories that center Asian perspectives and the winner of the 2016 Pulitzer Prize
- Tou SaiKo Lee: Writes music and poetry that blends hip-hop with traditional Hmong chanting
- Fred Korematsu: Challenged the legality of Japanese internment at the Supreme Court
- Kinney Kinmon Lau: Prevailed in a Supreme Court case that decided a lack of supplemental language instruction in public schools for students with limited English proficiency violated the Civil Rights Act of 1964

We who rise up

Guiding Questions
- Asians have a history of rising up against injustice. Why do you think we don't learn more about this?
- How can understanding our history strengthen our ability to speak out today?

Starting Points
- *Robert Bowne* ship mutiny of 1852
- Chinese Railroad Workers Strike of 1867
- Philippine-American War of 1899 and the Moro Rebellion
- Japanese Strike of 1909 in Hawaii
- Gurdit Singh and the Komagata Maru in 1914
- Japanese and Filipino interethnic strike in 1920 in Hawaii
- Helen Zia
- Asian American Political Alliance
- Asian Pacific Environmental Network
- #StopAsianHate
- The Asian American Foundation

We who stand in solidarity

Guiding Questions
- In what ways have Asians worked in solidarity with other marginalized and oppressed communities?
- Why are coalition-building and solidarity work necessary?

Starting Points
- Larry Itliong and the Delano grape strike in the 1960s
- Yuri Kochiyama
- Grace Lee Boggs
- Third World Liberation Front and the fight for Ethnic Studies in 1968
- Emma Gee and Yuji Ichioka
- Korean, Indian, and Filipino anti-colonial and national independence movements organized by exiles in the United States
- San Francisco Asian Women's Shelter

We who shine
Guiding Questions
- How are Asians reclaiming our narratives and defining our legacies?
- In what ways are we shaping the future?

Starting Points
- Alice Wong
- Alex and Eddie Van Halen
- Anna May Wong
- Carlos Bulosan
- Cecilia Chung
- Chanel Miller
- Connie Chung
- Dalip Singh Saund
- Fazlur Rahman Khan
- H.E.R.
- Hines Ward
- Indra Nooyi
- Jhumpa Lahiri
- Jose Rizal Elfalan
- Kalpana Chawla
- Kamala Harris
- Ke Huy Quan
- Maxine Hong Kingston
- Mee Moua
- Mia Mingus
- Min Chueh Chang
- Patsy Mink
- Peter Tsai
- Phillip Lim
- Prabal Gurung
- Roseli-Ocampo Friedmann
- Subrahmanyan Chandrasekhar
- Sammy Lee
- Sunisa Lee
- Tammy Duckworth
- Wat Misaka
- Yo-Yo Ma

. . . and spit it out
Guiding Questions
- How have Asians produced pearls throughout history?
- How are you producing pearls in your own life?

Starting Points
- Catarina de San Juan, "La China Poblana"
- Dith Pran
- Loung Ung
- Tereza Lee
- Sherry Chen
- Amanda Nguyen

We wear our iridescence
Guiding Questions
- What is the symbolism of textiles in many Asian cultures?
- How are these used to connect generations?

Starting Points
- Batik
- Chinese silk embroidery
- Kantha quilts
- Pandao story cloth
- Piña

We who produce pearls
Guiding Questions
- What does it mean to be Asian American? How can we explore and embrace the complexity and intersectionality of Asian American identity?
- How might we continue to strengthen a more unified Asian community? What are the challenges? What can we build on?

We have always
Guiding Question
- How will you rise up, speak out, step into power, and take up space?

We are children of the celestial
Guiding Questions
- What is your vision of the future?
- What is the impossible you will make possible?

Author's Note

While conducting research for this book, a wave of thoughts and emotions pummeled my soul. First, an intense anger over the total erasure of the history, pain, and triumphs of my people. I had never heard of a majority of these events or changemakers. We have been all but written out of the history we made possible.

Second, I felt a profound grief. Pain over the suffering we endured and continue to face. A mourning of what might have been had we known this history all along. How might we, as an Asian American community, unify if we could see how parallel our stories run? How might we, as a broader interracial community, stand together if we could see the ways we have always been used and connected throughout history? In unity and solidarity, we are powerful.

Finally, I felt an overwhelming sense of pride. I learned that contrary to stereotypes, we have always stood up, spoken out, and taken up space. We have always resisted injustice and fought for liberation. I felt a strong connection to those who have come before; we stand on powerful shoulders. Knowing this has allowed me to better access the power within.

Our book is a call to know our own histories in all their complexity and connectedness, heartache, and glory. We must seek out these truths. We must tell our own stories. We must harness the power of our ancestors, encase our truth in crystals, and drape ourselves in pearls. It is a call to stand together, with all the nuances and tensions and strength that exist in unity. It is a call to be proud. We are the constellations future generations will look to for light. We are the celestial. We were born to shine with brilliance so bright we rechart the course of the world.

This is an anthem for us.
— Joanna

Artist's Note

Joanna and I created this book for you, our vibrant Asian American community that has inspired us through shared stories and collaborative artmaking.

The past few years have been marked by violence, bigotry, and anguish. But I have witnessed how our community has kept us from being swallowed by the ugliness. I have seen us step forward and lead as public servants, educators, artists, and organizers. I have seen us demand our histories be taught and pass legislation to protect our most vulnerable. I have seen us open our restaurants, libraries, courtyards, and homes to hold space for grief, catharsis, and healing.

Borne from my own experiences as a misfit in the American South, I pay tribute to the nurturing yet imperfect life my immigrant parents granted me in *We Who Produce Pearls*. The journey through these pages will take you from serene rivers to amber waves and into soaring starlit skies. Let the words dance around you and the art embrace you in warmth and wonder. Immerse yourself in the textures, colors, and visions, and emerge with a burning desire to ignite the world with your unique radiance. To see yourself represented at last. To lead us all to liberation and joy, crafting a future unrestrained by what came before.

The generations before us cleared the paths we now walk. Their sacrifices echo in our blood and we now honor them by forging our own paths built on the foundations they have laid. If I have learned anything from the wisdom of our elders and foremothers, it is this:

We are more than the stories others have told about us. Beyond their labels and limitations. We sing life into being. We contain multitudes. We are stardust and seafoam, thunder and whisper.

This book is but a small offering — an invitation to dream and build alongside me. To acknowledge your limitlessness. And to always, always shine. You are the light keepers, the soul lifters, the world makers. Go forth and manifest wonders.

With heart,
— Amanda

For us.
— JH

To vibrant voices and resilient hearts:
may you be heard and healed.
— AP

Text copyright © 2024 by Joanna Ho
Art copyright © 2024 by Amanda Phingbodhipakkiya

All rights reserved. Published by Orchard Books, an imprint of Scholastic Inc., *Publishers since 1920*. ORCHARD BOOKS and design are registered trademarks of Watts Publishing Group, Ltd., used under license. SCHOLASTIC and associated logos are trademarks and/or registered trademarks of Scholastic Inc. • The publisher does not have any control over and does not assume any responsibility for author or third-party websites or their content. • No part of this publication may be reproduced, stored in a retrieval system, or transmitted in any form or by any means, electronic, mechanical, photocopying, recording, or otherwise, without written permission of the publisher. For information regarding permission, write to Scholastic Inc., Attention: Permissions Department, 557 Broadway, New York, NY 10012. • While inspired by and rooted in history, this is a work of fiction and some artistic and poetic license has been taken with the text and art.

Library of Congress Cataloging-in-Publication Data Available
ISBN 978-1-338-84665-2
10 9 8 7 6 5 4 3 2 1   24 25 26 27 28
Printed in China 62
First edition, April 2024
Book design by Doan Buu and edited by Clarissa Wong
The text type was set in Museo. The display type was set in Affogato.
The art was created digitally, using Adobe Illustrator.